YIRMI PINKUS

MR.FIBBER

BASED ON THE WORK OF
LEA GOLDBERG

FANTAGRAPHICS BOOKS, SEATTLE

MR. FIBBER
LOSES A COIN

DID YOU KNOW IT IS A FACT
THAT THE TRUTH IS NOT EXACT?

FACTS ARE CURIOUS, YES THEY ARE—
LIKE HOW I WOUND UP IN A JAR.

HOW I GOT IN AND THEN
HOW I MADE IT OUT AGAIN.

FROM THE START IT WASN'T PLANNED
I HELD THIS COIN IN MY HAND.

AND THEN, LIKE THAT, IT DROPPED SO FAR
INTO THE JUICE INSIDE THIS JAR.

I FOLLOWED IT AND TOOK A DIP
INTO THE JAR, QUICK AS A WHIP.

LIKE A DIVER IN THE SEA
TO RETRIEVE IT RAPIDLY.

IN THE WATER, WHILE I STOOD
GREAT GODS ABOVE! THIS WASN'T GOOD–

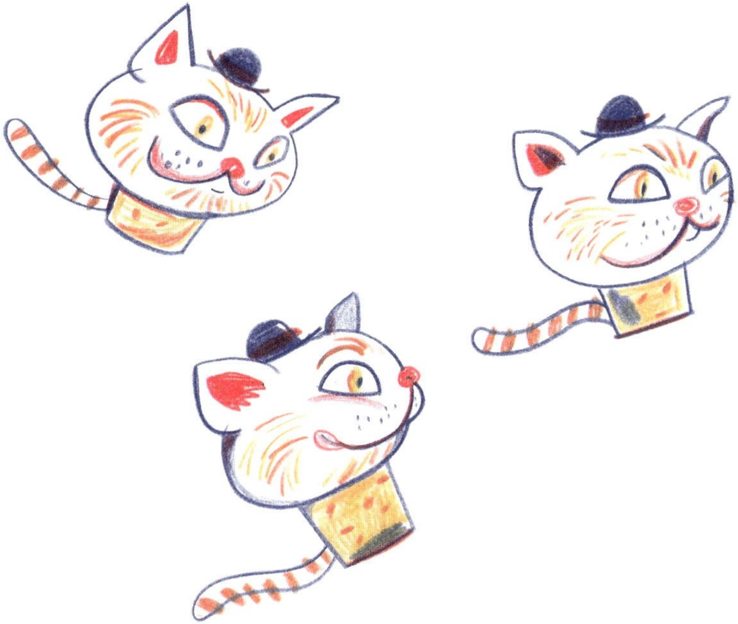

SOMEONE CAME BY IN A SNAP
AND CLOSED THE BOTTLE WITH A CAP.

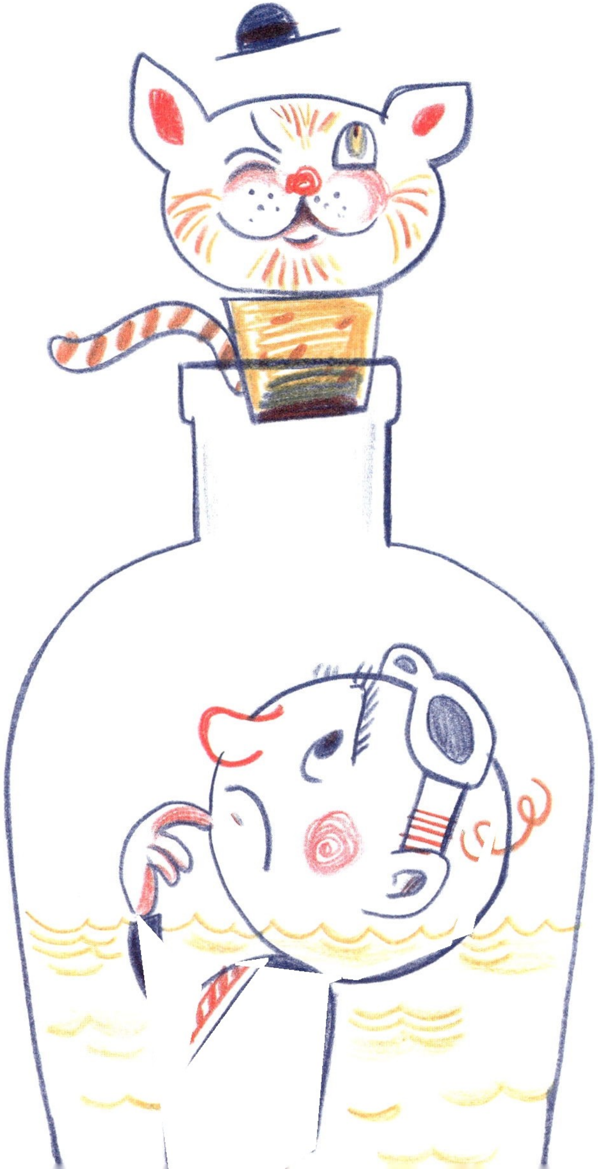

A DREADFUL MESS! WHAT WOULD I DO?
AND THEN WITH ALL MY STRENGTH I BLEW.

AND SO I HUFFED. I HUFFED AND PUFFED
UNTIL THE BOTTLE OPENED UP.

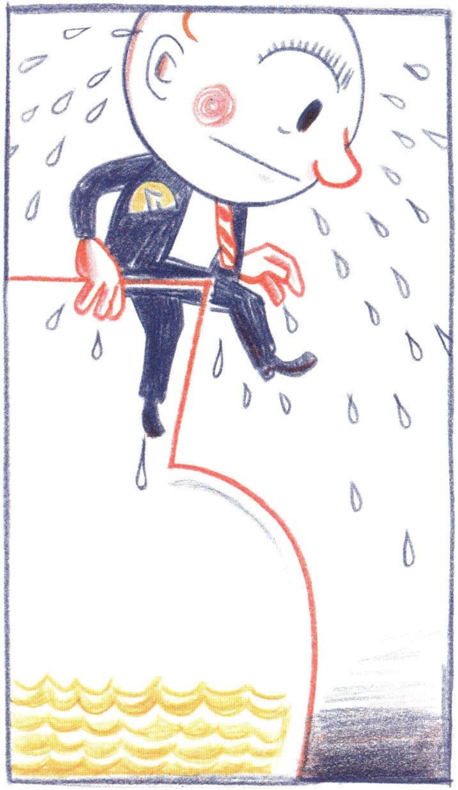

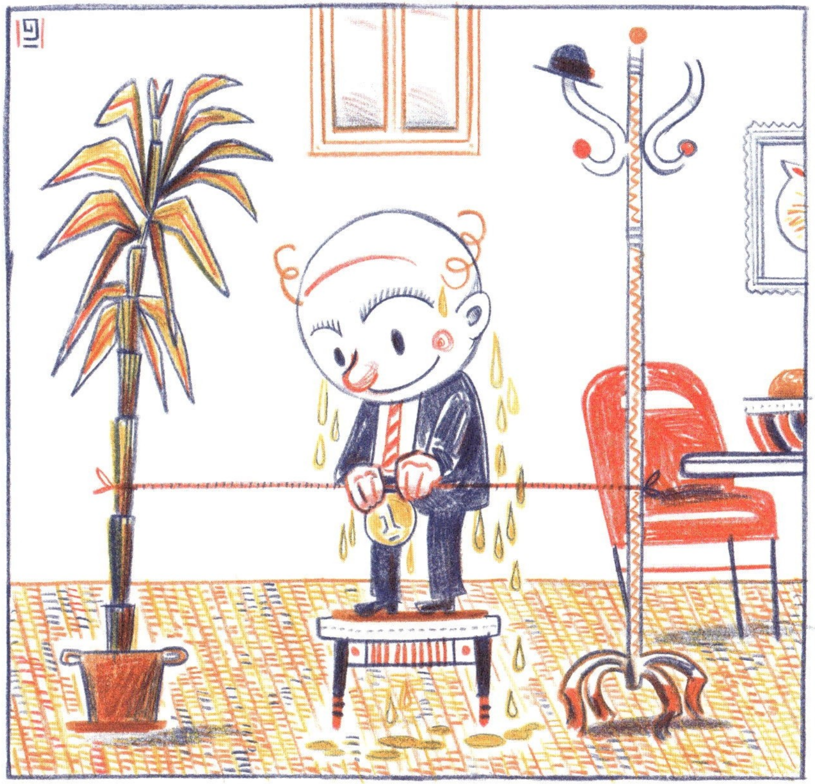

OUT OF THE BOTTLE, TO DRY LAND
I CLIMBED OUT WITH THE COIN AT HAND.

ALL IS WELL THAT ENDS WELL, AND YET–
THE COIN WAS STICKY, COLD, AND WET.

MR. FIBBER
ON THE TRAIN

MR. FIBBER SAID, HEAR YE,
THIS TALE IS WILD. YOU'LL AGREE.

WHILE I WAS WALKING ON MY WAY
A GIANT DOG CAME BY, A STRAY.

IT HAD EYES LIKE LANTERNS BRIGHT
AND WALKED THE TRACKS IN BROAD DAYLIGHT.

FROM ITS GREAT AND FURRY BACK
IT BILLOWED LIKE A GREAT SMOKESTACK.

THE DOG WAS HITCHED (DON'T BE AGHAST!)
TO A TRAIN CAR SPEEDING PAST.

SAID THE DOG, "SIR I INVITE
YOU ON MY TRAIN, SO PLEASE ALIGHT.

COME SIR, COME IN, AND TAKE A SEAT
ABOARD THE TRAIN, AND REST YOUR FEET."

SO AT ONCE I CLIMBED ABOARD
WITH NO CLUE WHERE WE HEADED TOWARD.

THEN SUDDENLY THE WHISTLE BLEW
AND IN A HURRY, OFF WE FLEW.

WE DROVE ON,

NO SIGN OF SLOWING.

I KNEW NOT

WHERE WE WERE GOING.

WHEN WE CLIMBED ATOP A HILL
THE GREAT DOG STOPPED AND ALL WAS STILL.

IT THEN REACHED DOWN INTO A HOLE
AND ATE A PILE OF DARK BLACK COAL.

AND THEN THE TRAIN WENT SPEEDING FAST
RIGHT BACK THE SAME WAY WE HAD PASSED.

WHEN I CAME BACK HOME AGAIN
I THANKED THE BIG DOG THERE AND THEN.
HE KINDLY BARKED, AS IF TO SAY
"COME RIDE MY TRAIN AGAIN SOMEDAY."

MR. FIBBER
AND THE SUN

MR. FIBBER SAID LAST NIGHT,

HEAR YE, FOR IT'S A FACT
I HAVE THE SUN, ALL HOT AND BRIGHT,
IT'S IN MY SUITCASE PACKED.

FOR TOMORROW OFF I GO
I'M HEADING OUT OF TOWN.

I WANTED TO MAKE SURE, YOU KNOW
THE SUN DOES NOT COOL DOWN.

FOR HOW NICE IT WILL BE TO REST
WHEN DAYS ARE WARM AND BRIGHT.

WITH SUNNY WEATHER, WE'LL BE BLESSED
AND HOT, CLEAR SUMMER LIGHT.

AND SO IN THE MID-AFTERNOON
I GOT INTO MY BOAT

YEAH!

AND TOOK THE SUN, 'TWAS NONE TOO SOON,
AND KEPT IT HERE AFLOAT.

I PACKED THE SUN
THAT I HAD PLUCKED

INTO A SHEET
ALL WRAPPED AND TUCKED.

AND NOW I'M HEADING OUT OF TOWN
MY FACE AGLOW AND BRIGHT—

HOORAY!

FOR THOUGH I'LL TRAVEL FAR AROUND
THE SUN WILL BE MY LIGHT!

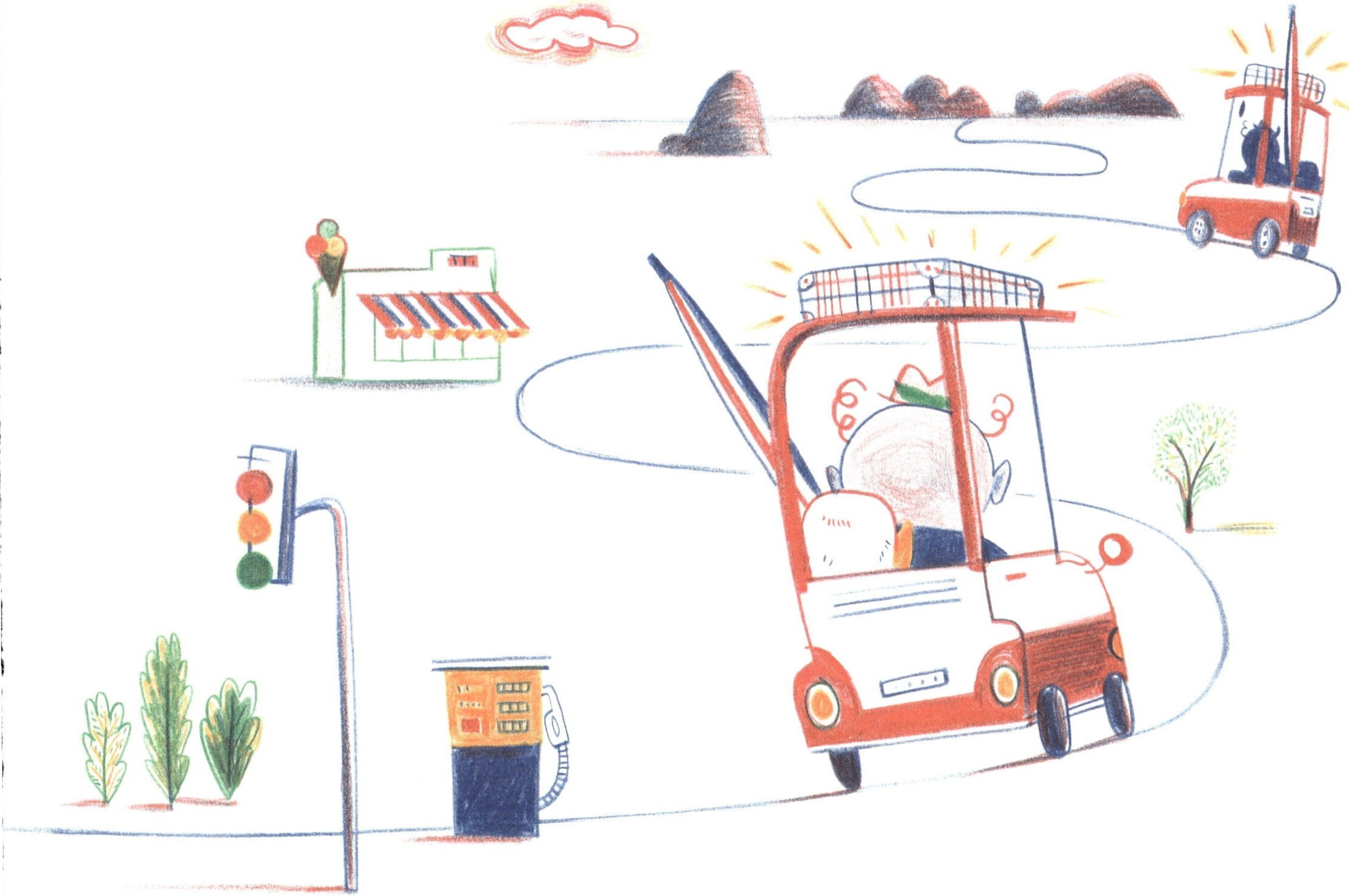

Translator: Ilana Kurshan
Editor: Conrad Groth
Designer: Jacob Covey
Supervising Editor: Gary Groth
Associate Publisher: Eric Reynolds
Publisher: Gary Groth

Fantagraphics Books, Inc.
7563 Lake City Way NE
Seattle, WA 98115

www.fantagraphics.com
Facebook.com/Fantagraphics
@fantagraphics.com

ISBN: 978-1-68396-178-9
Library of Congress Control Number: 2018949554
First Fantagraphics Books edition: February 2019
Printed in Malaysia